J.J. R___ and MON____

NICOLA MOON

ILLUSTRATED BY
ANT PARKER

KINGFISHER
BOSTON

To Rosalind—N. M.
To Cathy Carrot—A. P.

KINGFISHER
a Houghton Mifflin Company imprint
222 Berkeley Street
Boston, Massachusetts 02116
www.houghtonmifflinbooks.com

First published by Kingfisher in 1999
This edition published in 2005
2 4 6 8 10 9 7 5 3 1
1TR/0305/AJT/PW(SACH)/115MA/F

LIBRARY OF CONGRESS CATALOGING-IN-PUBLICATION DATA
Moon, Nicola.
J. J. Rabbit and the monster/by Nicola Moon; illustrated by Ant Parker.—1st ed.
p. cm.—(I am reading)
Summary: In separate stories J. J. suspects a monster when he finds large footprints
outside his burrow, and later he sets out with Mole and Squirrel to look for an adventure.
[1. Rabbits—Fiction. 2. Animals—Fiction.] I. Parker, Ant, ill. II. Title. III. Series.
PZ7.M776 Jj 2000
[Fic]—dc21
99-054154

ISBN 0-7534-5855-1
ISBN 978-07534-5855-6

Printed in India

Contents

J. J. Rabbit and the Monster

One morning J. J. Rabbit looked out
of his burrow. He saw some
footprints in the sand—great
big, round footprints.
He called out to Mole.

"Did you see who made
these great big, round footprints
outside my burrow last night?"
"No," said Mole.
"I was busy hunting
for worms."

J. J. called out to Owl. "Did you see who made these great big, round footprints outside my burrow last night?"

"No," said Owl. "I was flying over the fields."

J. J. called out to Squirrel.

"Did *you* see who made these

great big, round footprints

outside my burrow last night?"

"No," said Squirrel.

"I was away visiting my cousins."

"Wasn't *anybody* here last night?" asked J. J.
"Was I all alone?

All alone with a . . . with a . . .

MONSTER outside my burrow?"

He was beginning to feel a little

frightened.

The animals all studied the footprints.

"They're big," said Mole.

"They're round," said Owl.

"They're strange," said Squirrel.

"They're scary," said J. J.,

"and they're outside *my* burrow."

That night J. J. couldn't sleep.
He imagined all kinds of monsters
and giants clumping around,
making footprints in the sand
outside his burrow.
He tossed and he turned
until he was worn out.

Then he heard a strange noise.

Clump.

Clump.

Clump.

It grew louder and louder.

Clump.

Clump.

Clump!

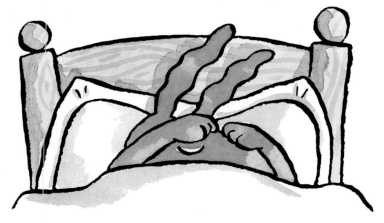

Now it was right outside his door.

Poor J. J. was too frightened to look.

He lay shivering under his blanket.

He was still there in the morning
when Mole came to find him.

"It came again!" J. J. told Mole.

"The *MONSTER* came again.
And I was all alone in my burrow.
Anything could have happened!"

J. J. was trembling to the tips
of his whiskers.

Mole called Owl and Squirrel over,
and they all studied the footprints again.

"They're very big," said Mole.

"They're very round," said Owl.

"They're very strange," said Squirrel.

"And very, very scary," said J. J.

The other animals agreed that the

footprints were very, very scary.

That night Mole, Owl, and Squirrel

decided to stay with J. J.

to try to see the Monster.

After dinner they all crowded

into his burrow.

Nobody was feeling very brave.

They waited.

Every time a twig snapped
or a leaf rustled,
J. J. dived under his bed.
They waited and waited
until Mole and Squirrel
were almost asleep.
Then they heard a strange noise.

Clump.

Clump.

Clump.

It came closer and closer.

Clump.

Clump.

Clump!

"It's coming to get me!"

squealed J. J.

"It's right outside,"

whispered Squirrel.

"Go and look,"

said Mole.

"No, *you* go and look,"

said Squirrel.

"We'll all go and look together,"
said Owl.
The animals crept toward the door.

Together they opened the door
a tiny crack,
just enough to peek out.
"What is it?" said Squirrel,
who didn't dare look.
"I don't know," said Mole,
her eyes tightly closed.
"It's a monster,
it's a monster!"
squealed J. J.,
his paws
over his eyes.

Owl was the only one
brave enough to look.
He flung open the door . . . .

"It's Badger!" he cried.

Sure enough, there was Badger.

He was carrying a huge bundle.

Clump.

Clump.

Clump!

went the bundle,

leaving big, round marks in the sand.

The marks looked *exactly*

like footprints.

"What are you doing?" asked Squirrel.

"I'm moving," puffed Badger.

"There's always so much . . .

stuff to carry . . . when you

move to a new house."

"J. J. thought you were
a scary monster," said Owl.
"He was frightened,
so we spent the night with him."
"*I* wasn't frightened," said Squirrel.

"Neither was I!" said Mole.

"It was only Badger, after all," said Owl.

"Yes," said J. J., looking at the marks that the bundle had left in the sand, "but it *could* have been a monster."

J. J. Rabbit and the Adventure

"I'm bored!" said J. J. one day.

"I feel like going on an adventure."

"An adventure?" asked Mole.

"What's that?"

"It's when you go somewhere new,

and something exciting happens,"

said J. J. "Owl told me."

"I think I feel like going on
an adventure too," said Mole.

"Let's go together!" said J. J.
as he scampered off into the woods.
"Wait for me!" called Mole.

They bumped into Squirrel.
"Where are you two going
in such a hurry?" he asked.
"We're looking for an adventure,"
said Mole.
"Looking for a what?"
asked Squirrel.

"An adventure," said J. J.
"It's when you go somewhere new,
and something exciting happens."
"Can I come too?" said Squirrel.
"Only if you don't run too fast,"
said Mole.

The animals followed a path
that twisted and turned
through the woods.

"Are we there yet?" panted Mole.

"Not yet," said J. J.

"How will we know when we are?"
said Mole.

"When we are somewhere new,"
said Squirrel.

"When something exciting happens,"
said J. J.

The animals walked until they
reached the end of the woods.

But they didn't find an adventure.

Then they walked past a field of wheat

and through a field of turnips.

But nothing exciting happened.

They walked for miles and miles.

They walked past a field of cows

and over a little bridge.

"I'm tired of looking for an adventure,"
said Squirrel.

"I didn't think adventures were
so far away," said Mole.
"Can we stop to rest now, J. J.?"
asked Squirrel. "J. J. . . .?"
Squirrel looked back along the path.

J. J. had disappeared!

Mole and Squirrel
looked behind trees . . .

and under bushes . . .

but there was no J. J.

Suddenly, Squirrel stood still.

"Listen!" he said. "What's that?"

"What's what?" said Mole.

"Ssshh!" whispered Squirrel.

33

A small voice was calling,

"Help! Help me!"

Mole and Squirrel followed the voice

back along the path to the bridge.

"Help!" it called again.

The voice was getting louder.

"It's J. J.!" cried Squirrel.

Mole and Squirrel looked

down over the bridge.

There was poor J. J.,

stuck in the mud.

"Help!" he squealed.

"I can't move!"

"It's all right," cried Mole.

"We'll save you!"

Squirrel found a long, strong stick
and held it out to J. J.

J. J. grabbed the stick with his paws
and held on tight.

Mole and Squirrel held the other end
and pulled.

And pulled . . .

and pulled . . . .

At last there was a loud

SQUISH!

and an even louder

PLOP!

and J. J. was free.

"Poor J. J.!" said Mole. "What happened?"

"I just came to get a drink." J. J. shivered.

"I didn't know the mud would be so

SQUISHY."

The sun was sinking
lower and lower in the sky.
It was starting to get dark.
"I don't want to look for
adventures anymore," said J. J.
"I just want to go home."
"I don't think there *are* any
adventures out here," said Mole.
"Which way is home?" asked J. J.
"Over the bridge, past a field of wheat,
and through a field of cows,"
said Squirrel.
"Or was it over the bridge,
past a field of cows,
and then through a field of turnips?"
said Mole, slowly.

"You mean you don't know?" said J. J.

"You mean we're *lost*?"

Mole shivered.

"I don't like being lost," she said.

"Especially not in the dark,"

said Squirrel.

"I want to go home!" wailed J. J.

It was getting darker and darker.

Suddenly they heard

a strange rustling noise.

"What's that?" whispered Squirrel.

"It's a wolf!" cried Mole.

There was more rustling,

followed by a swooshing noise.

"Help!" squealed J. J.

There was another swoosh,
and Owl swooped down from the sky.
"Oh, Owl!" said J. J. "We thought
you were a wolf! We're lost."
"Squirrel doesn't know the way
home," said Mole.
"And neither does Mole!" said Squirrel.
"Oh dear, oh dear," chuckled Owl.
"It's lucky that I flew by!"

Three very tired and bedraggled animals followed Owl as he led the way.

Soon they were almost home.

"Look, there's Badger!" said Mole.

Badger was sniffing around,

looking for slugs.

"Where have you all been?" he said.

"We were looking for an adventure,"

said J. J.

"But we couldn't find one," said Mole.

"We walked for miles," said J. J.,

"then I got stuck in the mud!"

"Then we got lost," said Squirrel,

"and Mole thought there was a wolf."

"But Owl came and saved us!"

cried Mole, happily.

"So you see," said Squirrel,

"there wasn't time for an adventure."

"No," said J. J., with a big yawn,

"but if we get up early tomorrow,

then we might find a *real* adventure."

About the author and illustrator

Nicola Moon used to be a science teacher, but now she writes books full-time. She says, "I hope readers will make friends with J. J. and his gang and enjoy sharing their adventures." Nicola Moon's other books for Kingfisher include the *I Am Reading* title *Alligator Tails and Crocodile Cakes*.

Ant Parker has illustrated many books for children. He doesn't know any rabbits, but he does know a monster who leaves big, muddy paw prints all over the house—his dog, Bramble. And Bramble looks just like Badger too! Ant Parker's other books for Kingfisher include the titles in the *Amazing Machines* series.

Strategies for Independent Readers

Predict
Think about the cover, illustrations, and the title
of the book. What do you think this book will be about?
While you are reading think about what may
happen next and why.

Monitor
As you read ask yourself if what you're
reading makes sense. If it doesn't, reread, look
at the illustrations, or read ahead.

Question
Ask yourself questions about important ideas
in the story such as what the characters might
do or what you might learn.

Phonics
If there is a word that you do not know, look carefully
at the letters, sounds, and word parts that you do know.
Blend the sounds to read the word. Ask yourself if this is
a word you know. Does it make sense in the sentence?

Summarize
Think about the characters, the setting where the
story takes place, and the problem the characters faced
in the story. Tell the important ideas in the beginning,
middle, and end of the story.

Evaluate
Ask yourself questions like: Did you like the story?
Why or why not? How did the author make the story
come alive? How did the author make the story fun to
read? How well did you understand the story? Maybe
you can understand it better if you read it again!